W9-ALN-628

Tabitha
The Fabulous Flying Feline

Carol Ann Timmel

Illustrations by Laura Kelly

Walker and Company
New York

To my dear friend Lacey
(who only chased cats for fun)
I miss you. —L. K.

First published in the United States of America in 1996 by Walker Publishing Company, Inc.

Published simultaneously in Canada by Thomas Allen & Son Canada, Limited, Markham, Ontario

Library of Congress Cataloging-in-Publication Data
Timmel, Carol Ann.
Tabitha: the fabulous flying feline/Carol Ann Timmel; illustrations by Laura Kelly.
p. cm.
Summary: When her cage opens accidentally during a flight to California, Tabitha the cat wanders off and becomes lost.
Based on a true story about the author's pet cat.
ISBN 0-8027-8448-8 (hardcover). —ISBN 0-8027-8449-6 (reinforced)
1. Cats—Juvenile fiction. [1. Cats—Fiction. 2. Lost and found possessions—Fiction. 3. Air travel—Fiction.] I. Kelly, Laura (Laura C.), ill. II. Title.
PZ10.3.T4496Tab 1996
[E]—dc20 96-13693
CIP
AC

Book design by Chin-Yee Lai

Printed in Hong Kong

2 4 6 8 10 9 7 5 3 1

Tabitha was a city cat. She lived on the fifth floor of a New York City apartment building with a young woman named Carol Ann, who had adopted her when she was just a kitten. They were the best of friends.

Tabitha liked to roll on her back and bask in the sun. And she loved to perch by the window to stare at the pigeons as they landed on the fire escape. She could watch children playing hopscotch in the courtyard below, but she was never allowed outside. Tabitha didn't mind; she was a scaredy-cat and didn't like loud noises or unfamiliar people.

NEW YORK

One day Carol Ann came home with a collection of cardboard boxes. Tabitha buried herself in the newspaper at the bottom of one of them. But Carol Ann filled Tabitha's boxes with clothes and dishes until all the apartment closets and cabinets were empty. Then big men came and took the boxes away, leaving only one behind. This box had holes in the sides and metal bars on the front. Tabitha recognized it right away. She didn't like it one bit, because it usually meant she was going to the vet.

Carol Ann was moving to a new home in California. "It's too far to drive," she told Tabitha. "We have to go on an airplane." Tabitha didn't understand a word of it, but she followed the smell of sardines into her cage.

When they got to the airport, Carol Ann put her face close to the metal bars and whispered, "Good-bye, Tabitha, fly safe." Tabitha had to fly in the cargo hold, because pets weren't allowed to ride with the passengers. When the plane took off, the jet engines were so loud they made Tabitha's ears hurt. So she buried her head under her paws and eventually fell asleep.

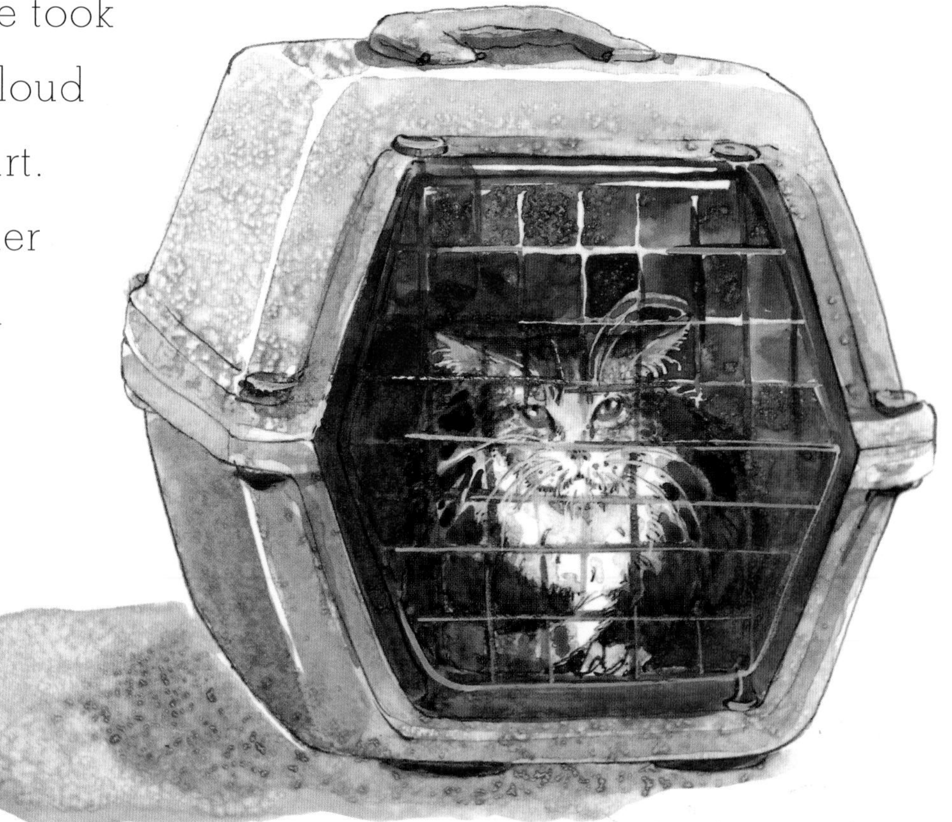

When Tabitha woke up, she was still on the plane . . . but her cage was open! She was sure she smelled fish. She followed the smell over to the crates of frozen salmon at the back of the cargo hold and rubbed her face along the edges of one box.

Just then the hatch door opened with a tremendous boom! Men in orange suits swarmed onto the plane. When they spotted Tabitha, they yelled and ran toward her. Terrified, she darted into an opening in the wall and squeezed herself into a ball.

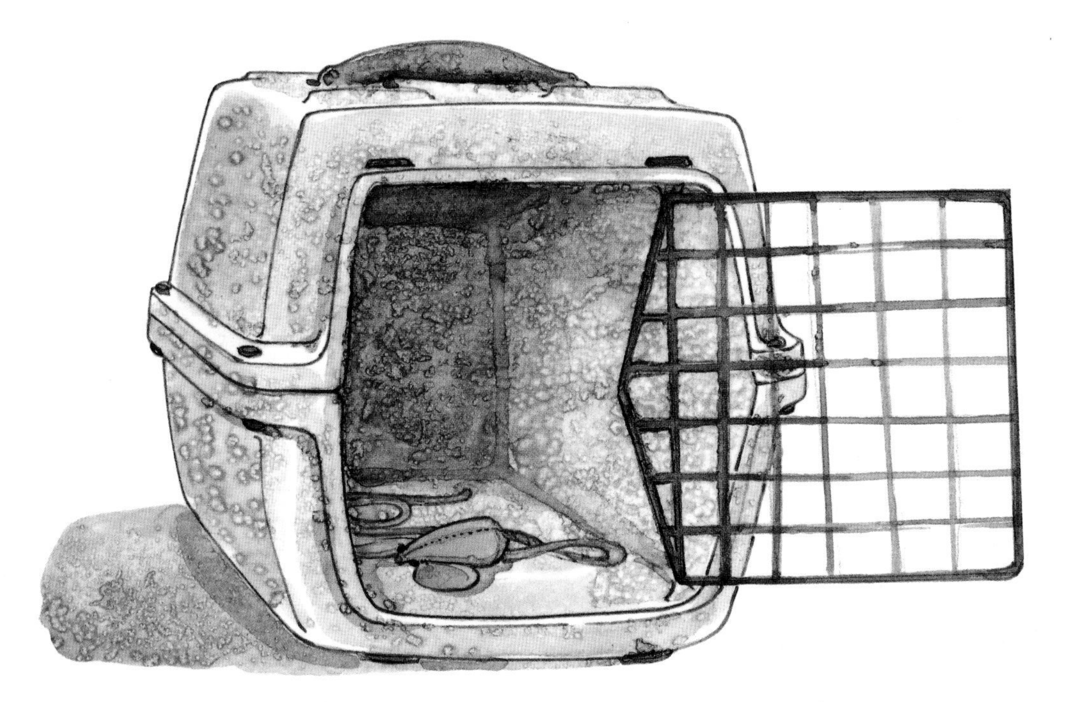

The minute she got off the plane, Carol Ann went to pick up Tabitha. First a dog was brought out. Then two cats came out, but they belonged to someone else. No Tabitha. Carol Ann began to get nervous. Finally, an airline clerk brought Tabitha's empty cage to her and told her that Tabitha was lost on the plane.

Carol Ann was horrified. "We have to find her!" she cried. "Please let me look for her. I know if she hears my voice she'll come out!" But the plane was already on its way back to New York with Tabitha on board. Carol Ann left for her new apartment alone.

From inside the wall of the plane Tabitha peeked through a trap door and saw people. Some of them were eating, some of them were reading, and some of them were sleeping. None of them were Carol Ann.

Then Tabitha peered through another trap door, this time above the cockpit. Carol Ann wasn't there either.

It was dark and narrow in the airplane walls and it was much quieter than the cargo hold. Tabitha crawled under some padding and fell asleep.

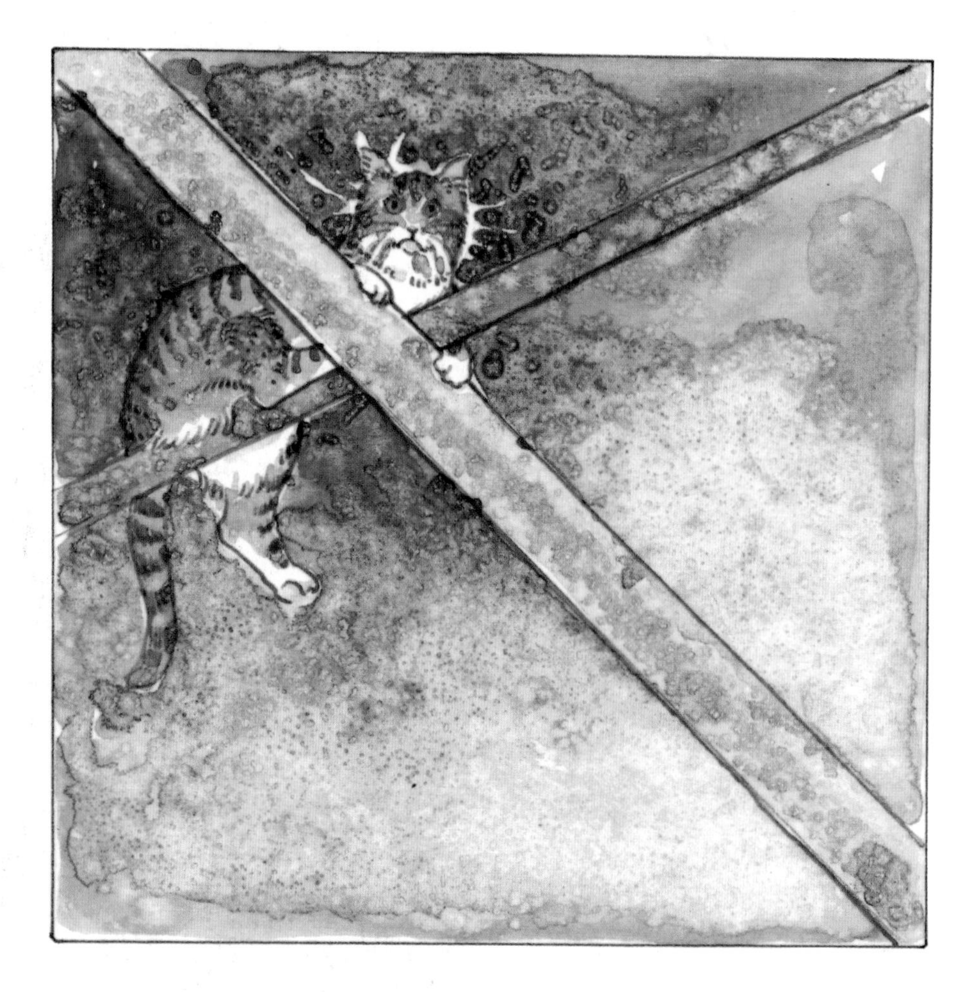

The plane took off and landed many times. Tabitha traveled to Puerto Rico, Miami, and Los Angeles. Every time the plane landed on the ground, it was very noisy.

Luggage and food were carried in and out. Trucks brought jet fuel. Men came and tested the engines. Mechanics came to work on the plane with big metal tools and flame torches. Cleaning crews came to vacuum. Tabitha hid from these loud people. She would never go to anyone but Carol Ann. But where was she? Had she forgotten her?

U-VAC
VAC

The people at the airline told Carol Ann that they were doing their best to rescue Tabitha, but she wanted them to do more. She didn't know anyone in her new city, so Carol Ann decided to ask the local newspaper for help. A reporter took her picture and wrote an article about Tabitha.

Soon Tabitha was in every newspaper and on every radio station in the country. Hundreds of people wanted to help find Tabitha. But the airline kept flying the plane every day. They would only let Carol Ann search the plane when it landed each night.

Night after night Carol Ann went to the plane to try to find Tabitha. She opened trap doors and called her name, but the engines were so loud that Tabitha couldn't hear her. Carol Ann asked the mechanics to turn off the engines and generators to make the plane quiet, but they weren't allowed to do that.

Tabitha was getting really hungry. She lapped water off some pipes when she was thirsty, but it didn't make her stomach stop growling. She should have stayed in the cage.

Carol Ann was very lonely in her empty new apartment. Every time she watched the news on TV she saw Tabitha's picture. When she turned on her clock radio, everyone was talking about her lost cat. It made Carol Ann miss Tabitha even more.

The airline didn't like what the reporters were saying about them. They finally agreed to ground the plane in New York for 24 hours. Many people were losing hope. How could Tabitha have lived for 13 days without food and water? But Carol Ann didn't give up—she flew to New York, determined to find her friend.

2GUYS WILL FLY U

The night the plane got very quiet, Tabitha was too exhausted to move. She could hear footsteps and tapping noises through the floors and walls. Then she heard a familiar voice call, "Tabitha? Where is my sweet tabby? Where is my little angel?" It was Carol Ann! Somehow Tabitha found the strength to let out the biggest meow of her life.

Carol Ann couldn't believe her ears. She decided to call again. "Where are you, my silly kitty?" Tabitha meowed again. This time, Carol Ann was certain that she heard her. She pushed up one of the ceiling panels and there was Tabitha!

Reporters swarmed all over as Carol Ann carried Tabitha off the plane. Tabitha was the fabulous flying feline who had survived for 13 days without any food.

While photographers snapped their picture, Carol Ann whispered to Tabitha, "If we ever move again, I promise we'll drive, no matter how far it is."